THE HAUNTED HOTEL

by Janet Adele Bloss

illustrated by Bill Robison

To the Callendar family—
Maddie, Keith, Sean, and Scott
and with special thanks to Bill Flynn in the White
Mountains of New Hampshire

Published by Worthington Press
7099 Huntley Road, Worthington, Ohio 43085

Printed in the United States of America
10 9 8 7 6 5 4 3 2 1

ISBN 0-87406-401-5

One

LAURA Bingman watched anxiously out of the car window as her father steered around an icy curve in the road. Suddenly, she saw it! Up ahead, the Royal Windmont Hotel came into view in front of a backdrop of rolling, white-capped mountains.

"Hey, look! There it is!" cried Laura. She leaned across her brother, Bill, so she could get a better look. "Wow. It's huge!" she exclaimed.

Bill pushed her back to the other side of the seat. "Quit crowding me," he muttered grumpily.

"You're such a grouch," whispered Laura. She turned away from Bill, and looked through the car's front window. Laura watched as the details of the big white hotel began to get clearer.

Glancing at her mother, Laura asked, "Do you think Uncle Joe ever gets lost in there?"

Bill snorted with laughter at her question. But Laura ignored him and waited for her mother's answer.

Mrs. Bingman smiled. "No, honey. I'm sure the other caretaker showed Uncle Joe around before he left," she said. "And remember that Uncle Joe has worked here for three months. He probably knows his way around the hotel pretty well by now."

"Gee," said Laura with a big sigh. "Look at how the sun reflects off the buildings. Isn't it pretty?" She gazed at the countryside around them.

"Yes, it really is something," agreed her mother.

"Wow," Laura said, leaning back into her seat. "New Hampshire is beautiful! I can't believe we're really going skiing here. This is going to be better than skiing in Michigan.

I'm glad that Uncle Joe got a job as the hotel caretaker."

"Me, too!" agreed her mom. "It will be great to visit with him and Aunt Gigi. And the fresh snow last night should make for some great skiing."

"I'll bet Aunt Gigi likes it here, too," Laura said as she picked up her Gwen Gilderstar mystery book from the floor. "I think it's cool that she moved in with Uncle Joe. I guess some brothers and sisters get along pretty well." Laura shot an accusing look at her older brother.

"Maybe Aunt Gigi doesn't drive Uncle Joe nuts," Bill said. "Maybe some sisters are okay. And," he added, "Aunt Gigi isn't in sixth grade." Bill said "sixth grade" like the words had a bad smell to them.

"What's wrong with being in sixth grade?" asked Laura angrily. "You think you're so great just because you're a year older than I am! It's only one year! Big deal!"

Mrs. Bingman looked from Bill to Laura.

"You know, you two, Gigi and Joe weren't always so close. I remember when we were growing up, they fought like cats and dogs. Joe used to tease Gigi about her red hair. And Gigi used to tease Joe about being so tall."

Laura fidgeted in her seat as her father drove the car up a small hill toward Uncle Joe's house. She watched as her mom studied a big map that she had spread out in front of her under the light in the car. "Turn left at the next road," her mom directed.

After a short ride up a curvy road, they stopped in front of a small wood-shingled house. Laura thought this house with fancy blue shutters looked just like a cottage from the fairy tales she used to read.

"Oh, boy. We're here!" shouted Laura. "All right!"

Bill winced. "You're so immature," he said. "Quit yelling. Uncle Joe and Aunt Gigi aren't deaf, you know."

Laura looked at her brother and frowned. "You think you're so cool just because you're

13," she complained.

Bill smiled one of his "I'm superior" smiles at her. "It's a lot better than being 12," he said.

"Ooo!" Laura groaned. "You're impossible!" She flashed her angry brown eyes at him. Then she pulled her knit cap down snugly over her ears and opened the car door. She climbed out of the backseat, stepping carefully onto the new snow.

Laura grabbed her small tote bag from the trunk of the car. Her father picked up her bigger suitcase. "What's in here?" he asked. "Rocks?" Laura laughed at her dad, who was pretending to fall over from the weight.

"Oh, Dad!" said Laura. "I just brought some Gwen Gilderstar books with me."

Laura tucked the Gwen Gilderstar book she had been reading under her arm and turned and ran toward the house. When she got to the front door, she saw that a piece of white paper was tacked to the mailbox. Laura pulled it down and read it.

Hi Sis, Jim, Bill, and Laura,
Come on in. I'm over at the Royal
Windmont Hotel doing a security check.
Make yourselves comfortable. I'll be back
soon.
Gigi isn't here. She left on an emergency
trip to Rhode Island to visit a sick friend.
She says "hello" and will try to be home
in a couple of days.

Joe

Laura waved the piece of paper in the air. "Aunt Gigi's not here!" she called to her parents. "I hope she's not gone more than four days, or we won't get to see her."

Mrs. Bingman sighed as she lugged a suitcase toward the house. "I haven't seen Gigi in months," she said. "I was hoping we'd be able to spend some time together, just skiing and talking."

Mr. Bingman came up behind her carrying two sets of skis. "Don't worry," he said.

"She won't be gone long. If I know your sister, she'll be dying to get together with you and tell you all the local gossip. I bet she's met some interesting people around here."

Laura smiled to herself because she knew exactly what her dad was talking about. Aunt Gigi always knew what was going on in the lives of people around her. And she wasn't shy about sharing the information. In fact, as Uncle Joe always said, "If you want to spread some news around, you can just tell Gigi."

Laura pushed the front door open and walked in. Bill was right behind her. "Look at that fireplace!" he exclaimed, looking around.

"Can we go to the hotel and look for Uncle Joe?" asked Laura eagerly. "I promise we won't bother him. We'll just walk with him while he does his security check."

Laura watched her mom's worried expression. "It's going to be dark soon," she said. "I don't know if you should go over there by yourselves."

"Please, Mom?" asked Laura. "We'll hurry

so we get there before it's dark. And then Uncle Joe will bring us back."

"What's this *we* stuff?" asked Bill. "What am I, your personal escort service? You know I'd never live it down back home in Indiana if my friends find out I spent my Christmas vacation hanging out with my sister."

"Bill, please go over there with Laura," asked Mr. Bingman. "I don't want your sister going that far by herself."

"Dad," moaned Bill. "Do I have to?"

Laura grinned as her dad nodded. Bill reluctantly pulled on his gloves and hat. Together they left the house and silently walked down the lane. Laura noticed that Bill seemed to be enjoying the walk, although he would never admit it. Turning a corner, they saw the huge hotel looming ahead of them. They followed the winding road that led up to the building. A sign beside the lane read,

THE ROYAL WINDMONT HOTEL
Built in 1899

"Wow! This place is old!" exclaimed Bill.

Laura nodded. "Yeah, it looks like something from a Gwen Gilderstar book," she noted. "I'll bet Gwen Gilderstar could find a mystery just by looking at this old hotel."

"I'll bet Gwen Gilderstar could find a mystery just by looking in a toilet," said Bill with a mischievous grin.

"You are so impossible," Laura protested. "Gwen Gilderstar is the very best detective in the whole world."

"She's just a character in a stupid book," said Bill. "I don't know why you take those things so seriously. There are no such things as mysteries with hidden boxes or ghosts or secret messages."

Laura pushed back her blond bangs from her forehead. "Oh, yes there are," she insisted. "Mysteries can happen any place and anytime. You just have to be ready for them!"

Bill shook his head and rolled his eyes.

"And you know what?" Laura continued. "The writer of the Gwen Gilderstar books lives somewhere around here. I read it on the cover of one of his books. It said that he lives in the White Mountains of New Hampshire, somewhere near Brinkley. Wouldn't it be great if we ran into him?"

"Ran into who?" asked Bill, as he walked closer to the hotel.

"Rutherford Thackeray," said Laura impatiently. "He's the man who writes the Gwen Gilderstar mysteries. Boy, I would love to meet him."

"So would I," said Bill. He scooped up a handful of snow and packed it into a ball. "If I ever meet Rutherford Thackeray, I'll make him eat a snow sandwich! Hey, you look kind of hungry."

"Get away from me with that snowball!" she yelled, laughing. "I mean it!" With a shriek, Laura ran the rest of the way up the hill. Laura could tell by Bill's noisy footsteps that he was galloping closely behind her.

When they reached the top of the hill, both of them stopped and looked around. "Wow," they both said at the same time.

The hotel stretched before them in a seemingly endless sweep of windows and chimneys. A wide gray porch went all the way around the outside of the hotel. The rooftop was a faded shade of red.

Laura listened and looked around. Her eyebrows drew together in thought. "That's funny," she said. "It's awfully quiet here. I don't see anyone around. Where are all the hotel people? Isn't anyone staying here?"

Bill listened as the evening wind whistled through the nearby trees. "Hmmm," he said. "That is kind of weird. Oh, well, let's check around."

Together, Laura and Bill climbed the porch steps and approached the front door. Laura turned the doorknob and pushed open the heavy oak door. She stepped inside into what seemed like a large parlor. The room was cold, dark, and silent. Laura peered around at the furniture covered in white sheets. A floorboard creaked as she walked across the room. A huge stone fireplace took up most of one wall.

She stepped back, gazing at the life-size portrait above the mantle. The woman in the painting was slender, and her black gown flowed to the ground. Dark hair swept across her shoulders and fell down her back to her waist. The woman held a bouquet of red roses in her arms. An emerald necklace sparkled from her neck. Her dark eyes stared out into the gloomy room.

"She's beautiful," whispered Laura. "I wonder where Uncle Joe is." Then, peering around, Laura whispered, "And where are all the people?"

"They probably all froze to death," said Bill with a shiver. "There's no heat in here." Puffs of cold air came from his mouth with each word. He glanced around the shadowy room, and then up at the portrait. "She looks like a vampire," he said.

"You're not afraid, are you?" Laura asked.

"Me? Afraid?" exclaimed Bill. He pulled back his shoulders and threw a punch at the air. "It would take more than a vampire to scare me!"

"It's dark in here," said Laura, a note of worry creeping into her voice. She reached toward the wall and flicked on a light switch. Nothing happened. "Oh, no!" she moaned. "There's no electricity! How are we going to find Uncle Joe?"

"You're not afraid of the dark, are you?" asked Bill.

"No, not me," said Laura, squaring her shoulders. "Come on. Let's look around this place for Uncle Joe."

Staying close to each other, Laura and Bill walked slowly from the hall into the next room.

"Whoa!" exclaimed Bill. "Take a look at this!"

Laura gazed around the formal-looking room. "Wow!" she exclaimed. "This must be a ballroom where everyone dresses up and dances." There were floor-length windows all around the room. A soft light reflecting from the snow outside came through the windows.

At one end of the room, there was a raised stage and a piano. Its black legs gleamed from beneath a sheet.

"Shall we dance?" asked Bill in a serious voice. Before she could answer, Bill did a spin on the shiny floor, and writhed and jerked his arms in a wild dance.

"You have absolutely zero class," Laura said, laughing. "It's getting dark," she added, looking nervously through the window onto the porch outside. "We'd better find Uncle Joe fast."

Laura and Bill left the ballroom and went back into the parlor, where the lady in black gazed down from her place above the fireplace.

Laura didn't want to admit to Bill that the empty old hotel made her feel jumpy. She turned her gaze away from the portrait. "Uncle Joe!" she called softly.

There was no answer. They walked through an open doorway into another empty room.

"I wonder why Uncle Joe never got married," Laura said quietly.

"He probably was afraid he'd get stuck with someone like you," said Bill.

Laura reached out and pinched her brother lightly on the arm. Then she called again, "Uncle Joe!"

Her voice echoed in the empty room and faded away. "Gee, maybe he's behind a secret panel or something," Laura reasoned. "Or, maybe he fell through a trap door. These old buildings always have secret staircases and stuff. In *The Mystery of the Disappearing Doll*, Gwen Gilderstar solved the mystery by finding a secret staircase behind some library shelves."

Laura ran her hand along the wood-paneled wall. She knelt on the floor and carefully looked at the baseboard, searching for hidden springs or hinges.

She glanced up to see Bill peering out a window. "Hey, Laura," he said. "I can actually see the sun moving."

Laura joined him by the window and watched the sun sink behind the top of a white mountain. In the next moment, the sun disappeared completely, and the room was plunged into shadows.

"Oh, this is great," moaned Bill. "Now I can't see a thing!"

"Maybe we'd better get out of here," said Laura nervously.

"I—I can't find the door," said Bill.

Laura reached her hand out into the darkness. She felt only empty air. Then, suddenly, her fingers touched something warm and boney. It felt like a hand—a very strong hand!

"Eeek!" shrieked Laura.

"Arrggg!" yelled Bill.

A beam of light flashed into their eyes as they found themselves face-to-face with a tall man with a big mustache.

"Uncle Joe!" they both exclaimed.

In the flashlight beam, Laura and Bill saw their uncle's smiling lips beneath his thick mustache. *Boy, is it good to see him,* Laura thought.

"I knew I heard someone down here," Uncle Joe said. "I was a bit startled, so I came down to check it out." He stooped and gave Laura a hug. Then he hugged Bill.

"I didn't scare you, did I?" asked Uncle Joe.

Laura shook her head. She didn't want to admit how much he had frightened her.

Uncle Joe swept the beam of his flashlight around the room. "This place sure is enough to give anyone the creeps," he said. "It's especially creepy when it's dark and empty. There are 250 rooms in the hotel. That can make you feel awfully alone."

"Where is everyone?" asked Laura.

"We close up in October," Uncle Joe explained. "This place is too big and old and drafty to heat through the winter. We'll open it up again in the springtime. The skiers stay in motels and cabins around town in the winter."

Laura and Bill followed their uncle into the front hall. Laura watched as her uncle's flashlight shone on the portrait over the fireplace.

The woman's pale face gazed down at them.

"Who is she?" asked Laura.

Uncle Joe hesitated before answering. "That's the princess," he explained.

"Well, who is she? Does she live here?"

"No, she lived here a long time ago," Uncle Joe said. "Come on, you two. I think it's time we get out of here for the night."

There's something weird about Uncle Joe, Laura thought. *He seems real jumpy, not like the old relaxed Uncle Joe I remember.*

Suddenly, Laura heard a faint thumping sound. "What was that?" she exclaimed. "I heard something upstairs! I heard footsteps!" Laura gazed up at the ceiling.

"It's just your imagination," said Uncle Joe anxiously. "Come on, kids. Let's get out of here." Looking nervously around, he said, "Listen, both of you, from now on, the hotel is off limits. It'll be better for everyone if you keep away from the hotel."

Uncle Joe opened the front door. As Laura turned to follow him, she gave a final glance at the portrait. She jumped as she saw the lady in black smile at her.

It's just my imagination, Laura thought. *I imagined the whole thing. Or, did I?*

Laura watched as Uncle Joe locked the heavy oak door behind them. It was then that she noticed that his hands were shaking.

Two

THE next morning was bright and sunny. *What a great day for skiing,* Laura thought. She followed her family from the Ski Hut, the local ski rental shop, and onto the cross-country snow trails.

"Wait up!" Laura called to her parents and Bill. She picked up her pace to stay close to them. Her father was leading the way toward the main skiing trails. He took big, smooth strides. Mrs. Bingman came next, gliding closely behind her husband. Bill followed with shorter, jogging steps.

The Bingmans came to a fork in the trail. A sign pointing to the left read "Horseshoe Trail." The sign pointing to the right read "Good Luck!"

"Does that mean you'll have good luck if you ski down this trail?" asked Laura.

"Or, does it mean you'll need good luck?" asked Bill.

Laura grimaced. She definitely did not want to ski down a trail head first. And the Good Luck Trail sounded a little scary.

Laura watched nervously as her father studied the signs. She breathed a sigh of relief as her father pointed a gloved finger toward the Horseshoe Trail.

"The Horseshoe Trail sign is green. That means it's a beginners' trail," he said. "It's better to begin with this trail and see how we do."

Laura skied next to Bill, letting her parents go on ahead of them.

"It's beautiful here," Laura sighed. "Everything's so perfect, except for one thing." She hesitated. "I wish Aunt Gigi were here."

Bill nodded. "I hope her friend gets better so she'll come back soon. I don't know, though," he added doubtfully. "Uncle Joe says that Aunt Gigi's friend is really sick."

Laura and Bill skied on in silence. They rounded a corner and found themselves looking down onto acres of rolling, snow-covered land.

"Look!" exclaimed Laura. Bill's gaze followed the direction of Laura's pointing finger. He shielded his eyes with his hand.

"Darn!" he said. "I can't see a thing. The snow's blinding me."

"Well, you should have worn your sunglasses," Laura said. She adjusted her tinted glasses and peered up at the huge building ahead of them. "It's the hotel!" she cried. "I can see it from here. Look! There's something in the tower. It looks like a person."

Squinting into the sunshine, Bill said, "I don't see anyone. It must be a glare on the window."

"No, it's not the glare," insisted Laura. "I know I saw something. There's someone up there!"

"It's probably just Uncle Joe," said Bill. "He's

probably over there doing a security check. After all, he's the only one with keys to the place."

Laura stood still, gazing intently at the hotel. "Now I can't see the shadow anymore," said Laura, squinting. "It's gone."

"It was probably just your imagination," said Bill.

Laura shook her head vigorously. "No," she said. "There was something or someone up in the tower." She thought to herself for a moment. Then, she added, "I wonder why Uncle Joe won't let us explore the hotel. Why doesn't he want us going near it?"

"Probably because it's full of ghosts and goblins," Bill said in a deep voice. He raised his hands into the air and pretended to be a monster. "Oooh! Ahhh!" he hooted in his best ghostly voice.

"Oh, cut it out," said Laura. "I'll bet we'd find a mystery in that hotel if Uncle Joe would let us look for it. It might be just like *The Case of the Whistling Attic*, where Gwen Gilderstar finds out that a gang of diamond thieves is hiding in an old attic."

Bill clapped his mittened hands together to keep them warm. "Yeah, sure," he said with big puffs of cold air coming from his mouth. "Or, maybe it's like *The Case of the Frozen Skier*, where Gwen Gilderstar freezes to death on a snow trail because she's so busy looking for mysteries to solve."

Laura rolled her eyes in response. "You have absolutely no imagination," she complained. "If Rutherford Thackeray was here right now, I'll bet he'd find a mystery in the hotel. He'd find a clue in the ballroom. Or, maybe he'd find a clue in the painting of the princess. Maybe there's a message in the painting. If we could just get in there and figure it out."

Laura cocked her head to one side. "You know," she added. "I'll even bet Rutherford Thackeray has seen this hotel before. After all, he lives somewhere around here."

Suddenly, with a swoosh and a spray of snow, three skiers came over the hill and glided toward her and Bill.

"There you are!" cried Mrs. Bingman. "We thought we'd lost you."

"Uncle Joe!" exclaimed Laura. "I thought you were over at the hotel! Wasn't that you in the tower window?"

Uncle Joe frowned slightly. "No, it wasn't me," he said. "I've been out here grooming trails all morning. That's part of my job here, too. No one's over at the hotel. It's all locked up." He jingled the keys in his pocket.

Laura turned her gaze across the snowy meadows toward the hotel. "But I saw someone," she insisted. "It looked like someone was in the tower window."

Uncle Joe's eyebrows lowered thoughtfully.

Bill made a circling motion with his finger next to his ear. "It's brain freeze," he explained quietly.

"No, it's not!" exclaimed Laura. "I saw someone! I really did!"

"Maybe it was the princess, and she's come back to haunt us," Uncle Joe suggested with a smile. "Folks around here claim that her ghost still walks in the hotel. Some of the hotel workers claim to have seen a woman in a long black gown who can walk through the walls." A grin tugged at the corners of Uncle Joe's mouth.

Laura's eyes grew big. She felt a shiver run down her spine.

"Oh, Joe," her mom was saying. "Don't encourage Laura. Her imagination is wild enough as it is."

Laura turned her brown eyes up to her uncle's face. "Tell me more about the princess' ghost," she begged. "Do you think she really could be in the tower? I bet Gwen Gilderstar would love to be here to solve this mystery."

Laura watched as her uncle pressed his mouth into a tight line. She wondered what he was thinking about. He seemed like he was about to answer, but then he stopped.

She was surprised when Uncle Joe grasped his ski poles and stepped back into the trail tracks. "I've got to get going," he said. "I have a lot of work to do." He glided forward and disappeared around a bend in the trail.

Mrs. Bingman sighed and looked down at Laura. She said, "Try not to bother Uncle Joe with so many questions. He has a job to do around here. Besides, you definitely have a wild imagination."

Laura didn't say a word. She glanced across the rolling acres of sparkling snow surrounding the hotel. The tower window seemed to be staring back at her. *I did see something in the tower, didn't I?* Laura asked herself. *No, it wasn't just my imagination! Someone was in the tower.*

Laura and Bill and their parents skied for the rest of the morning. They all stayed together on the beginner trails. By early afternoon, Laura and Bill took turns saying that they were hungry.

In the middle of a delicious hot sandwich-and-soup lunch at a busy diner in downtown Brinkley, Laura let her thoughts drift off to Gwen Gilderstar and the shadow in the tower.

What would Gwen do if she discovered something eerie like this? Would she just walk away? No way, Laura told herself.

And if there was a chance to do some more exploring in the big old hotel, Laura decided she was going to go for it.

"There she goes again, daydreaming," teased Bill. "She probably can see the ghost from here."

"I did see something when we were skiing. And you know it!" Laura said sharply. "Just you wait."

"Okay, you two. I don't want to hear any more about that hotel," said their mother. "Let's finish lunch and do some shopping around town."

They strolled through all the little shops in town. And later that evening, Laura sat in front of the big fireplace at her uncle's house. Laura's parents and Uncle Joe sat talking at a nearby coffee table. Laura had helped clean up the dinner dishes, and now she was massaging her aching leg muscles from her first day of skiing. Bill knelt on the other side of the hearth, whittling a stick with his pocket knife.

With a sigh, Laura returned to her book, *The Message in the Jewel Box.* She read how Gwen Gilderstar daringly crept into the basement of an antique store, even though the owners of the store were very suspicious and dangerous people. As she read further, Laura began to hear Uncle Joe's voice seeping into her thoughts. In her mind, she replayed his talks of the princess and her ghost.

After a few minutes, Laura heard Uncle Joe's voice from across the room. "I guess I'm just tired of hearing this stuff. But, since you all are so curious about it, I'll tell you a few more stories," Uncle Joe was saying to her mom. "The townspeople here actually believe that the princess' ghost haunts the Royal Windmont Hotel. Some of the summer workers claim to have seen her ghost up in the tower. Some of them refuse to go up there after dark! The caretaker before me even had a dog who wouldn't go into the tower. People say animals have a sixth sense about ghosts, you know."

Laura closed her book and moved closer to Uncle Joe, not wanting to miss a word. Bill closed his pocket knife and listened intently to his uncle's story.

"You see," Uncle Joe said, "the hotel was built by a French prince. The prince married a local girl who came to be known as Princess Marie."

"Was she a real princess?" asked Laura.

Uncle Joe nodded. "She sure was," he said. "That much I'm sure of. The front parlor where her portrait hangs is known as The Princess Room."

"She's so beautiful," sighed Laura.

Uncle Joe nodded. "Legend has it that her ghost can capture the heart of any man."

"It won't capture mine," said Bill. "I like girls who are alive."

Laura shot her brother an impatient look and turned back to Uncle Joe. "When did she die, Uncle Joe?" she asked.

Uncle Joe scratched his chin, and then he continued. "I think the prince died right after the hotel was built. And the princess died a few years later. That was about a hundred years ago."

Laura shivered with excitement. "Do you know any other stories about the princess?" she asked.

Uncle Joe shook his head. "I mostly hear gossip," he said. "People around here have lots of tales to tell about the princess."

"I'll bet Aunt Gigi would know all the gossip about the princess!" Laura exclaimed. "Aunt Gigi knows everything about everyone!"

Uncle Joe frowned slightly and looked into the fire.

"Please, Uncle Joe!" begged Laura. "Tell me everything you know about the princess."

Uncle Joe chuckled. "Okay," he said. "Who can turn down all this begging?"

Laura noticed that even her parents were smiling and waiting for Uncle Joe to continue.

She held her breath, waiting for him to start. Uncle Joe cleared his throat. "Well," he said slowly. "Some of the townspeople say that the princess locked herself in the hotel tower after the death of her husband. They say that she went insane in the tower. Other people say that she just disappeared one day and was never seen again. I'm not scaring you, am I?" asked Uncle Joe, looking anxiously at them. Laura and Bill shook their heads.

Uncle Joe continued. "The hotel gardener says that the princess' spirit walks through the rose garden in the summer. Roses were her favorite flower."

"She's holding red roses in the painting!" exclaimed Laura.

"That's right," said Uncle Joe.

"What other stories do you know about the princess?" asked Laura eagerly.

Uncle Joe thought for a moment. Then, he said, "One of the summer workers says that he saw her on an upper floor once. She was wearing a long black gown. I hear she crept up behind him and put her hands around his neck. He says that her fingers felt like icicles."

Mrs. Bingman glanced at her watch. "Ooops!" she exclaimed. "I guess that's it. I didn't realize it was so late. It's time for bed, kids."

"Can't we hear just one more story?" pleaded Laura. She turned her brown eyes to her uncle.

Uncle Joe looked at his sister to see if it was okay. Laura looked at her mom pleadingly until she finally nodded her head.

"Well, this is the last one then," said Uncle Joe slowly. "Hmmm. Let's see. Do you know the old woman who sells trail tickets in the Ski Hut?"

Laura nodded her head, recalling the short gray-haired woman behind the counter.

Uncle Joe continued, "Well, her name is Mrs. Natch. She's lived here in Brinkley all of her life. And she swears that the princess wanders the halls of the hotel, searching for just the right young girl. According to Mrs. Natch, the princess wants to take over a young girl's body so that she can come back to the land of the living."

Laura shivered at the thought of the princess taking over someone's body. A sudden thumping sound from outside caused the group to jump in their seats. Laura screamed and looked toward the window.

"It's just the snow," Uncle Joe explained. "It makes that sound when it slides off the roof."

Laura laughed nervously. Then, deep in thought, she said, "The princess sounds powerful. I wonder if she really went crazy in the tower." Laura clenched her teeth together. Even Bill's face looked serious.

"You kids aren't going to be able to sleep at all tonight," warned Mrs. Bingman.

"I'm not scared," Laura insisted.

"She thinks she's brave because she reads Gwen Gilderstar books," joked Bill. "She thinks she's a private detective."

Laura glared at her brother. Uncle Joe

leaned forward and picked up Laura's book. He stared at the title and at the author's name.

"It's written by Rutherford Thackeray," Laura informed him. "He's the best writer in the whole world! And he lives around here somewhere. I hope I get to see him before we have to go home."

"You'll probably run him down on the ski trail," laughed Bill.

Laura turned her back on Bill, determined to ignore him. "Do you know any other stories about the princess?" she asked her uncle.

Uncle Joe leaned back in his chair. A strange expression came over his face. "No more stories," he said suddenly. "I've told you kids too much already."

Suddenly, the phone rang, and Uncle Joe hurried to the kitchen to answer it. Laura stood up and stretched her legs. Then she walked down the hallway, pausing outside the kitchen door. She heard Uncle Joe say in a quiet voice, "Hi, Gigi. No, they're not here. They went out for dinner tonight. Yeah, sure. I'll tell them you called. Uh-huh. Gigi, I can't talk right now. Right. Good-bye."

Laura heard Uncle Joe hang up the phone. Why had Uncle Joe said that? Why did he want Aunt Gigi to think they weren't home? Laura decided that something really strange was going on. She hurried into the living room, where Bill was stabbing at the fire with a poker.

Laura watched Uncle Joe walk back over to the couch and sit down. "Who was on the phone?" her mother asked him.

Uncle Joe smiled nervously and said, "It was no one. It was a wrong number."

Three

LAURA and Bill set out early the next day, eager to hit the cross-country trails and do some exploring. Their parents had gone over to the downhill slopes and said to meet them later in the day. That left a whole day for Laura to see what else she could find out about the princess. She could hardly wait to get outside.

She and Bill headed first to the Ski Hut to get their trail passes. They leaned their skis against the posts outside and stepped inside the building.

Laura pointed to the gray-haired woman standing behind the counter who was handing purple trail passes to the skiers.

"That's Mrs. Natch," Laura whispered.

"Uncle Joe said that she knows lots of stories about the princess."

"Come on," said Bill, rolling his eyes. "Let's get the trail passes." Bill dug down into his pocket and pulled out $10. Laura followed him as he walked up to the counter.

Mrs. Natch smiled and said, "You must be Joe Kelly's niece and nephew. Joe and Gigi have told me so much about you two. I recognized you from your school pictures."

Laura smiled and stepped forward. "Uncle Joe says you know everyone around here," Laura said eagerly.

Mrs. Natch glowed with pride. Her eyes flashed behind her glasses. "Well, yes, I do," she agreed. "I've lived here all my life. I know just about everyone in Brinkley."

Laura took a deep breath. "Do you know Rutherford Thackeray?" she asked hopefully. "He's a famous writer. He writes the Gwen Gilderstar mysteries."

Mrs. Natch's forehead crinkled as she thought about Laura's question. "Hmmm," she said. "Rutherford Thackeray. Yes, I believe I have heard about him. It seems to me he's the fellow with the long white beard. He drives an old blue station wagon. I don't see him in town much. He must live up in the mountains somewhere."

Laura's heart jumped at the news that she was on the trail of her favorite writer. She had a lot more questions to ask Mrs. Natch, so she ignored Bill's impatient looks.

"Uncle Joe also said that you might know something about the princess," said Laura. "Have you ever seen her?"

Mrs. Natch gazed through a window in the direction of the hotel, and then she turned back to Laura and Bill. "Well, I've never seen her myself," she admitted. "But I do know plenty of people who have seen her. My husband used to work up at the hotel, and he says he saw her once up in the tower. He says she was moaning, and crying, and carrying on something awful. He says her eyes were glowing like fire, and her hair looked like snakes, all squirmy and squiggly."

Laura wrinkled her nose at the image.

"But," continued Mrs. Natch, "he says he saw her another time in the ballroom, and she was as pretty as a picture then. My husband believes the princess can change her looks whenever she wants to. When she wants to capture the heart of a man, she looks nice. But other times, she can look like your worst nightmare."

"What does she do once she makes a man fall in love with her?" asked Laura.

Mrs. Natch thought for a moment. She said, "Once a man is under her power, he'll do anything she tells him to do. The same goes for young girls. She'll cast her power over anyone who will let her. The princess isn't someone you want to mess around with."

Mrs. Natch pursed her lips into a grim line as Bill handed her the money to purchase the ski passes. Laura waved good-bye to Mrs. Natch, and she and Bill started walking toward the exit door.

Suddenly, Laura heard Mrs. Natch calling after her. "Now, don't you kids go playing around at the hotel! Ghosts aren't something to fool with, you know. Everyone around here knows that hotel is haunted. You keep away from there! You hear me?"

Laura and Bill stepped from the Ski Hut into the cold, bright snow outside. "See? I told you so," said Laura excitedly. "The hotel is haunted!"

Bill screwed his mouth to one side. "Don't believe everything you hear," he cautioned. "Maybe Mrs. Natch's husband just imagined that he saw a ghost."

Laura stepped into her skis and grasped her poles. "I think Mrs. Natch is telling the truth," declared Laura. She slid her skis over to the trail and began to ski forward. She looked back to be sure Bill was close behind her.

The bright morning sun had warmed the snow, making the trail icy and slick. At a fork in the trail, they stopped to read the trail signs.

One sign read "Upper Snake Trail." The other sign said "Lower Snake Trail."

"Either way, with the name snake, it looks like we're in for some fun," joked Bill. They picked the Lower Snake Trail for beginners, and they headed up, down, and around the trail's curves and hills.

As they glided around another curve in the trail, Laura's eyes grew big. "Look!" she cried.

Bill followed the direction of her finger. The Royal Windmont Hotel appeared just beyond a cluster of pine trees. Its chimneys thrust proudly up at the sky. The hotel had rows upon rows of windows, and they all looked black and creepy.

"I didn't know we were so close to the hotel," said Laura excitedly. "Come on. Let's go investigate!"

Bill hesitated. "We're not supposed to go in the hotel," he reminded Laura. "Anyway, we might get lost in there. Don't you remember Uncle Joe saying that there are more than 200 rooms in the hotel?"

Laura tossed back her sweaty blond hair. "What's the matter with you?" she asked. "Are you afraid of ghosts?"

Bill scowled at his sister. "No, I'm not afraid. Okay," he said. "Let's go. But we won't go inside. We'll just look through the windows."

Laura eagerly led the way across the ungroomed snow, through a field, and around the pine trees. Soon, they found themselves beside the huge porch.

Laura and Bill removed their skis and climbed onto the hotel's porch. "Shhh," she said to Bill, putting her finger up to her lips. She listened for a few seconds, but the only sound she could hear was the pounding of her heart.

"Look," said Bill, peering in one of the windows. "Here's the ballroom."

Laura joined her brother by a very tall window. Peering inside, she saw the black piano under its covering. The hardwood floor stretched into shadowy corners. Laura tried to imagine the hundreds of elegant balls that must have taken place in this room. She could picture the pretty women in their silk gowns and fancy jewelry.

Laura's imagination wandered further back through the years to a time when a pale woman in a black gown had waltzed across the floor in the arms of her husband, the prince. Perhaps the woman made a vow to herself that she would never leave the hotel. Perhaps the princess promised to stay in the hotel, even after death.

Laura felt Bill nudging her side. Reluctantly, she pushed the romantic and mysterious thoughts from her mind, and followed Bill along the porch. They passed window after window. Finally, they paused as they came to the heavy oak door that guarded the entrance to the hotel.

Laura reached for the doorknob and turned it. "Laura," Bill cautioned. "We're not supposed to go in the hotel."

"It seems to be locked, anyway," Laura said. She jiggled the doorknob. Suddenly, the door creaked open a few inches.

Bill stepped forward and peered inside the room. Laura didn't move. It was the same room they'd explored on the day they had arrived in Brinkley. But without Uncle Joe close by, Laura didn't feel quite so brave.

Bill slowly pushed the door open further and walked into the front parlor—The Princess Room. Laura stayed close behind him.

The huge portrait of the princess hung right in front of them. Laura studied the full-length portrait carefully. It seemed to Laura that the princess' eyes were looking straight at her.

Laura wondered if Gwen Gilderstar would be scared right now. *Probably not,* she decided. Laura pressed her lips together in determination. *Gwen Gilderstar isn't afraid of anything,* Laura thought. *I shouldn't be, either.*

Bill suddenly cocked his head to one side. "Did you hear something?" he asked.

Laura gulped and listened. She really didn't

want to hear anything, especially something scary. The sound of faraway music reached her ears. She and Bill looked silently at one another.

"It sounds like an organ," Laura whispered. Somber, deep notes floated from a distant room. A faint melody whispered, and then it faded. Then the music stopped.

Laura held her breath as another sound began. She heard clanking and grinding, squeaking and jangling. It sounded like chains rattling from somewhere deep in the heart of the hotel.

"Someone's dragging chains across the floor," whispered Bill nervously. "There's someone in here!"

"Do you think it's Uncle Joe?" asked Laura hopefully.

Bill shook his head. "Uncle Joe can't play an organ," he said.

"Who else could it be?" asked Laura fearfully.

They turned their eyes up to the portrait

on the wall. The princess stared down at them, a stony gaze from her piercing eyes. The woman in the portrait appeared to tremble. Then, suddenly, her face lurched forward as the painting fell from the wall. With a loud clatter and crash, the heavy frame hit the floor.

Bill and Laura jumped backward. "Let's get out of here!" shouted Bill.

With scrambling feet, Laura and Bill raced out the front door, down the porch, and stepped into their skis. Using all her strength to push herself with her poles, Laura struggled to catch up with her brother who was already up ahead of her.

Laura felt the back of her neck tingling with fright. Behind her, from somewhere deep within the hotel, she heard a sound. The faint echo of a woman's laughter floated after Laura as she and Bill skied desperately away from the hotel.

Four

"WHAT did I tell you?" asked Laura excitedly. "Didn't I say the hotel was haunted? Didn't Mrs. Natch tell us there was a ghost in the hotel? Now do you believe me?"

Bill pulled his hat from his head and twisted it in his hands. "I don't know what to believe," he admitted. "But all that stuff—the organ music, the rattling sound, and the picture falling off the wall—was definitely weird. I don't know what's going on And why was the front door unlocked? Do you think we should tell Uncle Joe about this?"

"Are you kidding?" exclaimed Laura. "We'd just get into trouble for going up there."

Laura and Bill caught their breath and exchanged glances before walking into Uncle

Joe's house. Their mom was sitting in a chair beside the fire. "Did you have a nice time skiing?" she asked with a big smile.

"Uh-huh," said Laura, thinking about all the ghostly things they had just witnessed. "I think I'll go to my room for a little while."

Laura knew her mother was looking at her strangely. After all, Laura never wanted to lay down in the middle of the day.

"Well, you do seem kind of tired," she said. "Maybe you should just rest for a while. We'll all relax tonight. Uncle Joe's taking us over to the Brinkley Motel after dinner. The owner lets Joe use the pool and the steam room. You packed your swimsuit, didn't you?"

Laura nodded and hurried from the room. She went to her bedroom and shut the door. She walked to her window and gazed out at the hotel at the top of the hill. Laura shivered as she recalled the ghostly laughter floating mockingly after her.

After dinner that night, the Bingmans crowded into Uncle Joe's jeep. He started the engine, and then drove down the lane and across a main street that led to the Brinkley Motel. As they climbed out of the jeep, Laura's nose stung from the cold night air.

Uncle Joe led the way to the swimming pool. A hot tub bubbled and steamed beside it. Around a corner was a door with a little window in it. Laura noticed a cloud of steam on the other side of the window and decided that it must be the steam room.

Laura and Bill swam in the pool while the adults soaked in the hot tub. Then Laura and Bill stood in the shallow end to talk.

"Maybe we should tell Uncle Joe," Bill whispered. "Since he's the security guard, he would want to know if someone's in the hotel playing an organ and rattling chains."

"He won't want to know about it if that someone's a ghost," Laura whispered back.

Laura and Bill climbed out of the pool and entered the steam room. Laura could feel the thick warm air fill her lungs. She sat beside Bill on a wooden bench. Around them thick clouds of white steam hung heavily in the air.

"What if it really was the princess?" Laura asked her brother. "Maybe she's trying to get a message to us." Laura fell silent for a few minutes. Then she said, "Maybe the princess knocked her own picture off of the wall."

Suddenly, a deep voice spoke from somewhere in the steamroom. "The princess isn't the only ghost," it said.

Laura jumped to her feet as a man's pale face appeared through the mist. Bill caught his breath. "Where did you come from?" Bill demanded.

The face moved closer to Laura and Bill. Steam curled around his jaws and rose from his shoulders.

"The hotel is never empty," the man warned. "There are spirits in that hotel just waiting for the right person to come along. Spirits attach themselves to living people. There are spirits in that hotel that are over a hundred years old. The older the spirits get, the more dangerous they become!"

Laura was speechless. She felt the blood drain from her face. The hair on the back of her neck stood up, just like it did when she heard the laughter coming from the hotel.

"The princess is the most powerful ghost," continued the man in the mist. "The other ghosts do what she tells them to do."

Laura moved slowly toward the door of the steam room. Bill followed closely behind her. Without a backward look, Laura threw open the door and rushed out into the clear cool air. She was relieved to see her parents and Uncle Joe still sitting together in the hot tub.

Bill looked back at the steam room. "That guy was crazy," he commented with a nervous laugh. But Laura could tell that her brother was shaken up, too.

"What's wrong?" asked Mr. Bingman, seeing Laura and Bill walk out of the steam room with strange looks on their faces.

"There's some creepy guy in there," explained Bill. "He appeared out of nowhere, and he started talking about ghosts and spirits and stuff. He was definitely a nut."

Uncle Joe frowned and climbed out of the hot tub. He crossed the floor to the steam room and disappeared inside. A moment later, he came out with a puzzled expression on his face. "No one's in there," he said, looking curiously from Bill to Laura. Then he grinned. "Are you sure about this?" he asked.

"Yes," insisted Laura. "He was in there just a minute ago."

"Well, he must have left while we weren't looking," said Uncle Joe. "Maybe it's time for us to leave, too."

After a shower and a change of clothes, Laura and her mom joined the others. Uncle Joe drove them back to his house.

Laura felt confused. As she got ready for bed, she thought about the strange conversation Uncle Joe had with Aunt Gigi on the telephone and about the ghost stories she'd heard from Uncle Joe and Mrs. Natch. And what about the organ music, clanking chains, ghostly laughter, and the weird man in the steam room? What did it all mean?

It was hours later that Laura's mind relaxed and she drifted into a sound sleep. Then, suddenly, she was awakened by the noise of a loud buzzer. Jumping from her bed, she ran into the hallway where she found her parents standing wide-eyed and confused. Bill burst from his bedroom.

Uncle Joe came running down the hall. "It's the security alarm at the hotel," he said. "Something's tripped a wire. I'd better get over there and check it out."

Laura watched as Uncle Joe punched a number code into the security alarm on the wall. The buzzing noise stopped.

"Do you want me to go with you, Joe?" asked Mr. Bingman.

"No, that's okay," said Uncle Joe. "The police get the signal at the station. I carry a gadget like a walkie-talkie, so they can hear everything that happens during the rounds. Besides, it was probably just a squirrel or a chipmunk. The alarm is a motion detector. It's only on at night, so if anything at all moves in there, the alarm goes off. I just need to check it out."

Uncle Joe's heavy boots clomped down the stairway. Laura felt comforted to be standing between her parents. Everyone repeated their good-nights and returned to their bedrooms.

But Laura couldn't sleep. She stood by her window, watching the headlights from Uncle Joe's jeep move along the twisting road up to the hotel. In the dark night, she could barely see him stop the jeep in front of the hotel. He left the headlights on. His flashlight beamed as he climbed the steps of the porch and disappeared inside the hotel.

Laura thought she could see the glow of Uncle Joe's flashlight as he moved room to room. The glow began in The Princess Room and moved on to the ballroom. Its light flickered behind the windows. Then, suddenly, the light disappeared.

Laura waited breathlessly by her window, her heart pounding. Nightmare visions filled her imagination. *What's happening to Uncle*

Joe? she wondered. She hadn't seen any police cars show up. Was he alone? Was a ghost waiting for him in the tower? Maybe he's screaming for help. What if the princess has him under her power?

Laura swallowed. Her eyes bugged as she strained to see what was happening. A light appeared at the hotel's front door. Laura sighed with relief when she saw Uncle Joe step outside into the glare of his jeep headlights.

Then, she gasped. Close behind Uncle Joe walked a dark figure. Uncle Joe turned and stood very close to the other person. Laura ran quickly from her room and tapped lightly on Bill's bedroom door. His sleepy voice asked, "What is it?"

Laura pushed the door open and whispered, "Come here. It's Uncle Joe. He caught someone in the hotel!"

Bill threw his covers back and stumbled out of bed. Running into Laura's room, he joined her by the window. Peering carefully into the darkness, he said, "I wonder who it is. The figure looks shorter than Uncle Joe. I think it's a lady, but I can't be sure."

Laura wished she had some binoculars. "It doesn't look like he's fighting with the person," she said. "If it was a burglar, wouldn't they be fighting?"

Uncle Joe's jeep pulled away from the hotel. Its headlights swept across the front porch before moving down the hill.

"Did she get into the jeep with him?" asked Laura.

"I don't know. I couldn't tell," whispered Bill.

"What are you kids still doing up?" asked Mr. Bingman. Laura and Bill jumped at the sound of their father's voice.

"We were just watching Uncle Joe," explained Laura. "It looks like he caught someone in the hotel."

"Really?" Mr. Bingman looked alarmed. He peered from the window, but by now Uncle Joe's headlights were hidden from sight.

Mrs. Bingman poked her head into the

room. "Isn't anyone sleeping?" she asked.

"Uncle Joe caught a burglar!" Laura exclaimed excitedly.

Her mother's eyes widened. She looked worried. "Should we call the police?" she asked.

Minutes later, the front door opened downstairs. Laura watched her mom rush toward the stairs. "Joe!" she called. "Is that you? Are you all right?"

Uncle Joe clomped up the stairs, brushing ice crystals from his jacket sleeves. "It's okay," he said. "It wasn't anything."

Laura piped up. "Did you catch her, Uncle Joe?" she asked.

"Did I catch who?" Uncle Joe asked, his eyebrows lowering. He paused. "There wasn't anyone there. It must have been a chipmunk that triggered the alarm."

Laura watched her mom's expression as she looked back and forth between Laura and Bill. "You kids!" she exclaimed shaking her head. "You have the wildest imaginations."

Mrs. Bingman turned to Uncle Joe. "The

kids thought that they saw you with someone," she explained. "They were sure you'd caught a thief."

Uncle Joe studied Laura's face carefully, and then he looked at Bill. He was silent for a moment. Then he said nervously, "No, I'm afraid I didn't. There wasn't anyone there. Good night, everyone. I'll see you all in the morning."

Uncle Joe turned and walked into his bedroom, closing the door behind him. Mr. and Mrs. Bingman disappeared down the hall.

Laura and Bill looked at each other.

"Why is Uncle Joe acting so weird? What's going on?" whispered Bill.

Laura gulped. "I don't know," she whispered back. "But maybe, just maybe—"

"What?" asked Bill.

Laura took a deep breath. "I bet someone's cast a spell on Uncle Joe," she said slowly.

"You don't mean...?" asked Bill.

Laura nodded. "Yes. It's the princess."

Five

"I don't think this is such a good idea," Bill warned Laura the next morning.

"Sure it is," Laura replied. "We've only got today and tomorrow left to solve the mystery. That's only two days. The only way to find out what's going on in the hotel is to investigate. It's the only way we can save Uncle Joe. He's been acting so weird, and it's because of the power of the princess."

Laura's voice sounded braver than she really felt. As they skied over toward the hotel, she kept a look out for a blue station wagon driven by a white bearded old man. Boy, would she like to see Rutherford Thackeray now!

They reached the hotel just a little breathless. Laura stepped out of her skis and leaned them against the front porch.

"What if Mom and Dad catch us here?" asked Bill.

"They won't," Laura said. "They're skiing. And Uncle Joe is out grooming the trails."

"What if the security alarm goes off?" asked Bill.

"It won't," Laura assured him. "It's only on at night. What's the matter? Are you afraid to go into the hotel?"

Bill shook his head vigorously. "No, I'm not afraid," he said.

Laura climbed the snow-covered steps to the porch. As she walked toward the front door, her heart began to pound.

She peered through a window into The Princess Room. "Someone put the picture back on the wall," she whispered.

"It was probably Uncle Joe," said Bill, gazing through the dusty glass pane.

Bill reached over to the front door and turned the knob. "It's locked," he said. Putting his shoulder against the door, he pushed.

"It won't budge," he said, huffing.

Laura and Bill walked around the hotel on the porch. They tried to keep their footsteps quiet. At each window, they stopped and peered inside the hotel.

"I wonder what it's like upstairs?" Laura asked. "And I wonder what it looks like in the tower."

"The tower?" asked Bill. "That's where the princess went crazy." He rounded a corner of the porch and gazed out onto the snow-covered lawns and tennis courts.

"Look!" exclaimed Bill. "That window looks like it's open."

Sure enough, when Laura and Bill looked closer, they saw that a window on the corner of the hotel was open just a bit. Pushing with all his might. Bill shoved the window upward. Laura felt her heart begin to race as Bill swung a leg over the windowsill and disappeared into the darkened room.

Taking a last look around her, Laura followed her brother through the window. She found herself standing in a large elegant dining room. There was a fancy glass china cabinet along one wall, and a crystal chandelier above her head.

Suddenly, Laura remembered the words of the man in the steam room. He had said, "The princess isn't the only ghost in the hotel. There are spirits in that hotel just waiting for the right person to come along. Spirits attach themselves to living people."

And then Mrs. Natch's warning replayed itself in Laura's head. "The princess isn't someone you want to mess around with. No, not her! You keep away from that hotel! Everyone around here knows it's haunted!"

Laura took a deep breath and then walked quickly to catch up with Bill. The only sound in the hotel was their footsteps echoing through the empty old corridors.

Laura stepped out into the hall. It was hard to see anything in the darkness.

"Did you bring a flashlight?" asked Laura.

"No, Laura. Did you?" asked Bill defensively.

Laura ignored his comment and continued to tiptoe down the hall. The light shining in from the big windows in the front hall made everything easier to see. Suddenly, The Princess Room was before them.

The princess' long dark hair flowed down over her shoulders. Laura thought about the person she had seen with Uncle Joe the night before as she looked at the portrait. Laura wasn't sure about the length or color of the person's hair. It had been too dark to see very clearly.

Laura continued to gaze up at the princess. Her face looked beautiful and frightening at the same time. Her dark eyes peered down. Laura felt like the princess' eyes were following her. "What's this?" asked Laura. Dashing forward, she gazed down at a red rose lying on the floor under the portrait of the princess. She picked it up and saw that the tips of the petals were slightly wilted and curling. But the bottom of the petals remained velvety soft and fresh.

"Where'd that come from?" asked Bill, coming over to get a better look.

"It was here by the painting," explained Laura in a trembling voice.

"That looks just like the roses in the picture!" exclaimed Bill. "I don't like this, Laura. There's something going on around here."

Laura lifted the rose to her nose. She breathed in a faint, rosy scent. "This rose isn't very old," she whispered. "Someone must have put it here recently."

Carefully, Laura placed the rose back where she found it. What would Gwen Gilderstar do if this was happening to her? Laura wondered. Laura knew that Gwen would be brave and wouldn't give up. She'd search for every possible clue and then add them up to solve the mystery. She'd save Uncle Joe from the ghost and its power.

With a deep breath, Laura led the way to the staircase. It spiraled upward into the shadowy floors above.

Stairs creaked under their weight as Laura

and Bill slowly climbed upward. As they reached the second floor, there was a strange noise. Laura peered down the hallway, trying to figure out where the noise had come from.

It was a faint noise that sounded like *peep-peep-peep*. It peeped and then stopped, peeped and then stopped.

With a nervous laugh, Bill pointed at the ceiling. "It's the smoke alarms," he said with relief "The batteries must be dead."

Laura glanced down the hall at the smoke alarms that dotted the ceiling. She grinned at her brother. "That's good detective work," she complimented him. "Come on."

Laura and Bill slowly climbed the stairs to the next floor, and then they continued to the next. They walked down a hallway and glanced into the rooms. Laura wrinkled her nose. "It's not very nice up here," she said. "This must be where the employees stay in the summer. The guests get the good rooms downstairs. Look, Bill! It's some kind of flashlight!"

Laura bent to the floor and picked up a

small black flashlight. It was a little rusty, but when she flicked on the switch, a faint light streamed out the end of it.

"Hang onto that," said Bill. "We might need it later."

She gulped and said, "Come on. Let's go up to the tower."

Bill didn't say a word. He walked with Laura back down the hall and up the stairs. The next floor up was the top floor. Laura found herself staring at a ladder on the wall. The ladder stretched upward to a trap door in the ceiling.

"This must lead to the tower," whispered Laura. She felt the small flashlight in her pocket.

Laura set her foot on the bottom rung of the ladder. She hesitated, remembering the story about the princess locking herself in the tower after her husband had died.

"I'll go first if you're afraid," offered Bill.

"N—no," stammered Laura. "I'll go. I'm the one who got us into this."

Laura's legs felt like lead as she climbed the ladder. At the top, she pushed at the trap door. It didn't budge. Then, using both hands and all her strength, she pushed it again. This time the door creaked open. Laura gripped the floor above her head. Pulling herself upward, she thrust her head and shoulders into the tower room.

Her eyes needed a minute to adjust to the darkness. There was one window in the tower. And for some strange reason, it was high up near the roof.

Heaving herself upward, Laura scooted onto the tower floor, and then she stood up. A moment later, Bill was standing beside her.

Bill whispered, "Everyone says this is the most haunted room in the hotel."

Laura felt the hair on the back of her neck and arms prickle. Shadows crowded in around her. Thrusting her hand into her coat pocket, she pulled out the little black flashlight and switched it on. She noticed that the batteries seemed to be growing weaker.

"Oh, no!" whispered Laura. "The flashlight is going dead."

She tried the switch once more. It cast a dim light around them. Laura saw boxes and something shadowy beyond the boxes. A strong gust of wind clattered at the window and seeped into the drafty tower.

"What's that over there?" Bill asked.

Laura held the flashlight's tiny golden light in the direction of Bill's pointing finger. In front of them was something so horrible that it took their breath away. It was so frightening that for a second they couldn't even move.

Is this real? Can this really be happening to me? Laura asked herself. Laura's scream echoed through the tower. Bill grabbed her arm. In the dim, wavering glow from the flashlight, Laura and Bill saw her at the same time.

She stood in a corner of the tower in a black gown. Her long dark hair straggled over her shoulders. Her wild eyes stared out at them from a pale, bloodless face.

It was the princess!

Six

THE princess stood perfectly still. Laura's heart felt as if it were being squeezed tight with fear. Laura leaned closer. The feeble light from her flashlight flickered across the princess' white face.

Suddenly, Laura's hands went stiff with fear. The flashlight fell to the floor, flickered, and went out.

"I can't see!" Laura yelled. She was trying hard not to panic. "Bill, come on. Let's go. We have to get out of here fast!" Turning, she quickly made her way toward where she remembered the trap door was.

"Laura, wait!" Bill's hands scrambled for the flashlight Laura had dropped. With trembling hands, Bill shook the flashlight, and the

feeble light appeared again. Slowly, Bill turned the light into the corner where they had seen the princess.

The next sound Laura heard was laughter—crazy laughter. It took Laura a minute to figure out that the laughter was Bill's.

"Bill, are you nuts?" Laura asked in a shaky voice. "Let's get out of here."

"Laura, look," Bill said, shining the light into the corner. It's just a painting of the princess. It's not her at all."

"Another painting?" Laura asked. She summoned up all of her courage and looked toward the dark corner. Sure enough, it was a life-size painting. But it wasn't nearly as beautiful as the one downstairs in The Princess Room. This painting looked hideous—as if it was from an advertisement for a horror movie.

Laura shook her head. These clues just didn't make sense.

"Come on," Bill said. "This place gives me the creeps even if it was just a painting we saw. Let's get going."

Laura opened the trap door and climbed to the floor beneath. She heard Bill climbing down behind her.

"Do you want to get out of here?" Bill asked nervously.

"N-no. Do you?" Laura asked.

"Uh, no. For Uncle Joe's sake, let's look around some more," Bill suggested.

They huddled close together as they walked down the hallway. The hall was lined with closed doors. Bill threw open one door after another, sticking his head into each room. Cold drafts of air burst into the hallway as he opened each door. Laura pulled her knit scarf more tightly around her neck.

"Hey, Laura! Come over here!" Bill yelled as he disappeared into a room. Laura followed him.

Laura joined him beside the window. Her eyes scanned the floor where he pointed.

"Look! Footprints!" exclaimed Bill with excitement. "And, they're fresh! Someone must have just made them!"

Laura's head reeled at the sight of another clue. There, before her eyes, was a thin layer of snow on the ground beside the window. In the very center of the sparkling snow were two small footprints.

"High heels," Laura mumbled. "Those prints were made by a lady."

Bill looked curiously around the room. "What I can't figure out," he said, "is how snow got into the room when the window is closed. And," he added, "whose footprints are they? Could they belong to the princess?"

Laura felt a shiver run through her. She shrugged her shoulders, not wanting to think of the frightening possibilities. "Maybe we should go tell Mom and Dad," she suggested hesitantly.

"Are you kidding?" hooted Bill. "They'd kill us! We're not even supposed to be here, remember?"

"Well," suggested Laura. "Maybe we should just forget the whole thing."

Bill frowned at Laura. "Are you wimping out?" he asked accusingly. "You're the one who started this whole thing! What about saving Uncle Joe from the power of the ghost? Don't you care about him anymore?"

"Of course, I do!" exclaimed Laura defensively. "But it's so creepy in here."

Again, Laura thought about what Gwen Gilderstar would do in a situation like this. Gwen never backed away because she was scared. She kept going until the mystery was solved and everybody was happy again. Laura knew she had to do that, too.

As they made their way through the hotel, a sound came floating down the hallway.

"Oh, my gosh!" Laura exclaimed under her breath. "That's the same laughter I heard yesterday when the picture fell off the wall!"

Bill stood perfectly still, and Laura could tell that he was frightened. A pulse throbbed in his neck.

"Someone's in the hotel," he said softly.

"It could be the princess!" whispered Laura.

Laughter bubbled from somewhere in a distant area of the hotel, and then it faded into silence. Laura caught her breath as she thought she heard the sound of clanking chains.

The clanking sound grew louder and louder. Bill grabbed Laura's hand. "Come on!" he urged.

Laura ran with Bill into the hallway. Laura turned to race away from the sounds of the chains, but Bill caught her elbow. "This way!" he whispered. He turned a corner in the hallway, and with his finger against his mouth he warned Laura, "Shhh!" With his other hand, he pointed to the door of an old freight elevator that ran without electricity.

"Someone's coming up here!" Bill whispered.

"Let's get out of here!" urged Laura. She hung back, watching in alarm as her brother pressed his eye against the crack in the elevator doors.

"Bill!" Laura squealed.

"I've got to see who it is!" Bill insisted.

As the elevator came closer, its chains shook and shivered under its great weight.

The grinding of gears became louder as the elevator reached their floor and continued on. Bill stared through the crack in the door as the elevator hesitated and then passed by, disappearing into the floor above.

Bill turned around slowly, and Laura saw that his face was really pale. The courage he had just moments before was gone.

"It was the princess," Bill whispered, his teeth chattering. "It was really her!"

Laura felt her heart drop into her shoes. She waited for Bill to say something else.

Bill's eyes bugged out as he said, "She wore a long black dress. And her hair was long, just like in the painting. And she was carrying a silver ax."

Laura felt her skin go tight with goose bumps and fear. Without a word, she turned and ran down the hall. Taking the steps two at a time, she raced down four flights of stairs.

The sound of clattering behind her told her that her brother was close on her heels.

Laura choked back a scream as she saw that the rose by the painting was gone. She cast a quick glance up at the princess' portrait. The dark eyes stared down as mysterious and haunting as ever.

Laura raced across the floor and tugged at the front door. It wouldn't budge. Then, remembering that they had come in through a window, she ran into the back room. She saw with relief that the window was still open. Throwing a leg over the sill, Laura climbed out onto the porch. She fell and rolled onto her shoulder. Bill heaved himself through the window and slipped on the icy porch, falling to his knees.

Quickly, they scrambled to their feet. Running around the porch, they found their skis and poles stuck into a snowdrift where they had left them.

Slipping her feet into her skis, Laura grabbed her poles and pushed herself away from the hotel. Her brother glided along beside her.

We'll be lost in the snow! Laura's mind whirled with deadly possibilities. The princess will come after us, and everyone will think we're still out on the trail!

They stopped at the edge of the woods to catch their breath. Bill turned to his sister. "I can't believe it!" he shouted. "I saw the princess! She exists!"

Seven

"NOW, remember," Bill said shakily as he stacked his skis in Uncle Joe's garage. His arms were still trembling a little. "Don't say a word about being near the hotel. If we get in big trouble now, there's no way we'll be able to help Uncle Joe."

"I know," Laura nodded. "Why don't we ask him to tell us some more about the princess and the hotel tonight after dinner? Maybe he'll slip in something important."

"Hey, that's a good idea," Bill said. "Maybe we'll be able to tell if she has a spell over him." He pulled the garage door down, and they went inside for lunch. After a meal of steaming soup, Laura and Bill went into the backyard for a snowball fight. Actually, it started as a snow-man-building project, but soon Laura had coated Bill's jeans with snowballs.

Later that evening, after reading a few chapters of her Gwen Gilderstar book, Laura went upstairs and knocked on Bill's bedroom door.

"Come in," Bill called.

"Mom and Dad are with Uncle Joe downstairs by the fire. Come on. Let's go down and see if Uncle Joe will tell us anything," Laura said.

Bill pulled a sweater over his T-shirt and then followed Laura downstairs. They joined the rest of the family by the fireplace.

"Do you know any more stories about the princess Uncle Joe?" asked Laura eagerly.

Mrs. Bingman smiled. "I'm afraid my kids have a great appetite for ghost stories," she said.

"Come on, Uncle Joe!" urged Bill.

Uncle Joe's voice was reluctant. "Well," he said. "There's one story I haven't told you. One of the summer guests said she saw the princess sitting on her bed one night. She said the princess laughed and then vanished into thin air."

Laura and Bill exchanged a meaningful look.

"She laughed?" asked Laura.

Uncle Joe nodded. "People say she smiles and laughs and floats through the halls. Some say she's as pretty as an angel. You have to admit that she's pretty," he said. "That long black hair and her dark brown eyes are just beautiful."

Laura thought of the black-gowned woman Bill had seen in the mechanical elevator that afternoon. "Do people ever sneak into the hotel when you don't know it?" she asked.

"It's not likely," said Uncle Joe. "I've got the security alarm on at night. And I patrol the hotel during the day. The place is locked up well."

The telephone rang. Before Uncle Joe could answer it, Laura jumped up and ran to the kitchen. "Hello?" she called into the receiver.

"Laura? Is that you, honey?" Aunt Gigi's voice sounded clear, but far away.

"Aunt Gigi!" exclaimed Laura. "Where are you? We're only going to be here one more day. Are you coming home?"

"I'm still in Rhode Island," Aunt Gigi said sadly. "I was just calling to talk to Joe. I'm hoping he won't mind if I come home so I can see all of you before you leave."

Laura could hardly believe her ears. "What?" she asked curiously. "Why wouldn't Uncle Joe want you here? I thought you had a sick friend."

"Is that what he told you?" Aunt Gigi asked. "Why, that rascal! He practically threw me out of the house. He insisted I go visit a friend I'd been eager to see. But she's not sick. I just came for a friendly visit because Joe insisted I do. Hmmm. Joe's been acting pretty strange lately."

Laura lowered her voice. "I think so, too, Aunt Gigi," she admitted.

Laura heard footsteps approaching from

behind her, and she glanced over her shoulder. Uncle Joe stood in the doorway. "Who is it?" he asked.

"It's Aunt Gigi," answered Laura. As Uncle Joe reached for the phone, Laura stepped backward. "I'll just talk for a minute," she said.

Uncle Joe frowned and stood silently, waiting.

"I'd love to see you," said Aunt Gigi. "And I've got so much to tell your mother." Laura smiled as her aunt chattered on with all the local and family gossip.

Uncle Joe shifted his feet impatiently. Laura noticed a worried expression on his face. After a few minutes, he walked down the hall.

Laura clutched the telephone receiver in her hand. "Aunt Gigi," she whispered, "do you know anything about the hotel? Have you noticed anything strange about it?"

"Well, yes," said Aunt Gigi. "I have seen some strange things. Joe goes over there at the strangest times. And he gets fidgety if I ask him what he's doing there. He seems to ignore me sometimes, like he's in a trance. And lately he seems really nervous about something. Frankly, I am worried about him."

Laura darted a look at her uncle, who had come back into the kitchen. He stroked his dark mustache and frowned.

"When are you coming back?" asked Laura.

Suddenly, Uncle Joe reached for the telephone. He took the receiver from Laura. "Hello? Gigi?" he called heartily into the phone. "How are you?"

Uncle Joe cupped a hand over the mouthpiece and turned to Laura. He whispered, "I have something personal to ask Gigi."

Laura nodded and left the kitchen. She closed the door behind her. But instead of rejoining her family in the living room, Laura pressed her ear against the door. She could just make out what Uncle Joe was saying.

"Not yet, Gigi," he said. "The furnace isn't working very well. It's cold as the dickens here! Yes, and you know how long it takes you to

get over bronchitis. You'd better not come home yet until it's fixed. No, the others went out for some night skiing. Laura's the only one here. Uh-huh."

There was silence, and then Uncle Joe exclaimed, "No, Gigi, not tomorrow! Gigi!" There was another silence, and then Laura heard her uncle hang up the phone.

Laura hurried into the living room. Her mind whirled with what she had just heard. There's nothing wrong with the furnace. So, why did Uncle Joe lie? Why didn't he want Aunt Gigi to come home? He never used to be like this. What's wrong with him?

"Who was on the telephone, Laura?" Mrs. Bingman asked.

"It was Aunt Gigi!" Laura said cheerfully.

Mrs. Bingman jumped up from the sofa. "Gigi?" she exclaimed. "That's wonderful!" She turned toward the kitchen just as Uncle Joe walked into the family room.

"I'm sorry," said Uncle Joe. "She had to run. It was some sort of emergency with her sick friend. She said to say hello to everyone."

Mrs. Bingman looked disappointed.

"She'll be home tomorrow," Uncle Joe added.

"She will?" Mrs. Bingman's face brightened with a smile.

"Yes," said Uncle Joe finally.

Laura approached the fire and whispered to Bill. "Come upstairs. I have something to tell you."

Bill yawned and stretched. "Gee," he said. "I think I'll go to bed. All this skiing really tires a guy out."

Laura yawned widely. "Me, too," she said. "I need some sleep after all this exercise."

Mr. Bingman smiled. "Good night, you two," he said. "Are you sure you don't want to try some downhill skiing with your mom and me tomorrow? It's our last chance to ski together."

Laura shook her head. "I'll stick to cross-country skiing," she said. Bill nodded in agreement.

As Laura walked up the stairs with Bill,

she heard the adults start talking again.

"It's too bad Gigi had to stay away for so long. She said her friend was very ill," Uncle Joe said.

"He's lying!" Laura exclaimed under her breath when they reached her bedroom. Bill pulled a chair away from the wall and sat down, listening to what his sister had to say. When she finished repeating the phone conversation she'd heard, Bill wiped a hand across his forehead.

"Whew!" he said. "Uncle Joe's in worse shape than I thought. "Either he's going nuts, or—"

"Or, he's really in her power," Laura finished. "Uncle Joe is haunted by the princess!"

Eight

LAURA spent a sleepless night sorting out the clues in her mind. There was the laughter she'd heard in the hotel and the painting that flew off the wall. Then there were the weird stories told by Uncle Joe, Mrs. Natch, and the mysterious man in the steam room. All the stories agreed on one thing. They all said that the ghost of Princess Marie continues to live on in the hotel, even though she died nearly a hundred years ago.

Laura forced herself to think more about the mystery. After all, time was running out, and Uncle Joe's future was at stake. He just wasn't the same Uncle Joe anymore. He was always nervous, and he lied about the strangest things. Why did he send Aunt Gigi away?

Why did he lie to her about the furnace not working? Why didn't he want Aunt Gigi to talk to us? Did Aunt Gigi know something that he didn't want us to hear? Did she suspect that he was in the power of the princess?

Laura thought it was weird that Uncle Joe wanted to keep her and Bill away from the hotel. He had to be hiding something over at the hotel. He had to be!

Laura thought about more mysterious clues. There was the spooky organ music that floated out from nowhere and the red rose that lay beneath the painting in The Princess Room. There was the hideous painting of the princess in the same tower where the princess had gone crazy. And what about the lady's footprints in the snow? And how did snow get in through a closed window?

One by one, Laura sifted through the clues. She tried to explain them. She tried to find logical explanations for each ghostly event. But, there was one clue that could not be explained.

"Bill really saw her!" Laura whispered to herself. "He saw her in the elevator, and she looked just like the woman in the painting!"

Laura grew tired as she mulled over the mystery of the princess. Dawn finally approached as she fell into a fitful sleep. She was awakened by a knock at her door. Mrs. Bingman stuck her head into the room. Laura saw that her mom was already dressed for skiing.

"Are you sure you don't want to try some downhill skiing with us today?" her mother asked. "Your dad and I want to get an early start. After all, we leave to go back to Indiana tomorrow."

Laura sat up in bed. Rubbing the sleep from her eyes, she said, "Go ahead, Mom. Bill and I are going to try out a different cross-country trail today."

Mrs. Bingman smiled. "I think it's great the way you two have been getting along," she said. "I guess this vacation has brought you two together."

Laura knew her mother wouldn't be so happy if she knew a ghost was the reason they were spending so much time together.

"Uncle Joe will be in town for most of the day," Mrs. Bingman said. "He has work to do over there. So, why don't you meet us at the house for a late lunch. How about around two o'clock?"

"That sounds fine, Mom," Laura said.

Laura heard her mother's footsteps going down the stairs. A short time later, the car engine roared outside as her parents took off for the slopes in the next town.

The grumble of another engine brought Laura to her feet. Who could that be? Maybe Aunt Gigi was home already.

Laura ran barefoot across the cold floor to the window. Looking down, she saw Uncle Joe's jeep backing out of the driveway. *I guess he is going into town like Mom said*, Laura thought.

Laura watched as he drove down the road and disappeared from sight. Then a moment later, the jeep reappeared as it climbed the twisting road to the Royal Windmont Hotel.

Laura ran from her room and dashed into Bill's bedroom. He was curled up under layers of blankets. Laura shook him until he woke up.

"Bill!" she exclaimed. "Uncle Joe's going over to the hotel to see the princess! He told Mom he was going into town. But he went to the hotel. He's acting weird again. Come on. We've got to go save him from the ghost!"

Bill jumped out of bed. Laura ran back to her room and quickly stepped out of her pajamas and into her clothes. Moments later, she met Bill at the top of the stairs, where they galloped down two steps at a time.

Laura threw on her jacket. "Let's walk up the road. It's faster than skiing across the fields," she said.

Side by side, they jogged down the lane, slipping along on the packed snow and ice.

"Look!" Laura pointed to a battered blue station wagon slowly making its way down the road. A bearded old man sat behind the steering wheel.

"It's Rutherford Thackeray!" shrieked Laura. "He's appeared right when we need him the most!"

"Who?" asked Bill.

"He's the mystery writer! He'll know what to do. Maybe he can help us." Laura threw her hands into the air and waved wildly as the old blue car approached. "Stop!" Laura shouted.

The car slowed and then stopped. Laura saw with excitement the lined, bearded face of the driver. He rolled his window down, looking curiously at Laura. "What's the matter?" he asked in a creaky, tired voice. "Do you kids need a ride somewhere?"

Laura shook her head vigorously. "Please, Mr. Thackeray," she pleaded. "You've got to help us. We're in the middle of a mystery!"

The old man recoiled in alarm. He stared suspiciously at Laura and Bill. "What's wrong with you kids?" he asked.

"Nothing's wrong with us," Laura said

excitedly. "It's just that we thought you could help us solve a mystery since you're a mystery writer. You are Rutherford Thackeray, aren't you?"

The old man shook his head. "I'm afraid you've got the wrong person," he said. "I'm Willard Phelps. And I'm definitely not a writer."

He frowned as he rolled his window back up. A moment later, his blue station wagon disappeared down the road. Laura stared after him. "I guess Mrs. Natch was wrong about the blue station wagon," she said. "It's not Mr. Thackeray's car, after all."

When they finally reached the hotel, they saw Uncle Joe's jeep was parked in front of the hotel.

Bill headed to the front door and shook the knob. "It's locked," he said grimly.

"We'll use the window again," said Laura.

Laura and Bill pushed together on the window. After a final tug, it slid upward. Laura hurriedly climbed through the window into the dining room. She sniffed gingerly at the air. Then, in a frightened voice, she whispered, "I smell roses!"

Bill breathed in deeply. Then he nodded, fear in his eyes. "She must be somewhere nearby," he said in a hushed voice. "Maybe she already has Uncle Joe in her clutches."

Laura and Bill tiptoed from the room into the hallway. They stood quietly, listening for any sounds. Suddenly, there was the echo of faraway laughter.

"It's the princess," Laura whispered.

The laughter was followed by the sounds of clanking chains.

"She must be in the elevator," said Bill. "Come on!"

Together they ran down the hall toward the elevator shaft. Bill peeped through the crack in the door. "It's going up!" he exclaimed.

Laura and Bill galloped up the spiraling staircase. At the next floor, they ran down the hall. Laura's heart quaked as she looked to her left and saw a wild-eyed face staring out from under a mop of blond hair. Then Laura realized she was staring into a mirror.

They raced down the hallway until at last they stood again by the elevator shaft. The jangling and cranking sounds from the gears were growing louder, and then they were quiet again as the elevator passed by and continued to climb. The sound of soft female whispering floated from the elevator, and Laura felt the hairs on the back of her neck prickle from fright.

Bounding down the hall, Laura and Bill climbed the next set of stairs. Rushing to the elevator, they listened and waited as it slowly, haltingly approached and then continued upward. A man's deep voice came floating down.

"She's going to the tower!" Laura exclaimed. "And she's got Uncle Joe!"

Laura and Bill raced up the next flight of stairs and then the next. On the top floor, they waited, panting, by the elevator doors.

They have to stop here. We're going to see the princess face to face! What will she do to

us? Should I jump on her? Can you wrestle with a ghost?

The old mechanical elevator trembled and stopped. Laura caught her breath as she waited for the doors to open. Silence came from the elevator, and Laura wondered if the princess might have vanished into thin air.

Slowly, the elevator doors opened. Laura saw her uncle standing there, his eyes round with shock, as if he were in a trance. As he stepped forward into the hall, the woman behind him came into view.

"It's her! It's the princess!" Laura shrieked. Laura flinched as she looked at the face of a ghostly-white woman with long flowing hair. The woman's brown eyes darted rapidly from Laura to Bill.

And in her arms the woman held a big bouquet of red roses.

Nine

LAURA stood frozen with fear. She glanced over at Bill. His face had gone pale, and his eyes looked glazed over with fear.

Without a second to spare, Laura screamed, "We'll save you Uncle Joe!" But Uncle Joe just stared blankly at her.

What was wrong with him?

Laura felt so powerless against the powers of the ghostly princess. *Couldn't Uncle Joe see that the princess could hurt her and Bill, too? Didn't Uncle Joe care?*

The princess' eyes loomed dark and scary. Suddenly, she recoiled in horror, shrinking eerily back into the darkness of the elevator.

"Let's get her, Bill! Come on!" yelled Laura.

Bill and Laura tried to dodge Uncle Joe and

make a wedge between him and the evil princess.

"Don't worry, Uncle Joe!" Laura shouted. "We'll save you from her powers."

Laura stepped menacingly toward the woman in the elevator. Laura was scared, but seeing her uncle in the clutches of an ancient ghost spurred her to action.

"Leave Uncle Joe alone," growled Laura.

"Yeah!" shouted Bill as he stepped forward. As he moved closer to the elevator, Uncle Joe caught him by the collar. He put his arms to stop both of them from going near the princess.

"Stop it! Hold on there," Uncle Joe said.

Bill darted a hopeless look at Laura. "Oh, no," he moaned. "It's too late. He's completely in her power."

Uncle Joe looked confused as he held his niece and nephew at arm's length. He looked back at the princess, who still stood rigidly at the back of the elevator.

Then, in one movement, the princess

stepped forward. She held out a pale hand. "You must be Laura," she said.

Laura was frozen in place. She inspected the mysterious princess from head to toe and noticed that she wasn't wearing a black velvet gown. She was wearing a long black winter coat.

Uncle Joe cleared his throat. He glanced apologetically at her. "I guess it's time to clear up this mess," he said. "The secret is out."

The woman nodded as Uncle Joe said, "Laura, Bill, I'd like you to meet my fiancée, Pam Jones."

"What?" Laura felt confused. She looked from her uncle to the woman. Bill just stood there looking confused.

Uncle Joe grinned. He put his arm around the woman's shoulder. Laura noticed that his arm didn't pass right through her the way it would pass through a ghost. Was it possible that this was a real flesh-and-blood person? Or, was she just a really sneaky ghost?

Uncle Joe saw their startled expressions

and laughed. The woman beside him laughed, too. Laura shivered as she realized this was the same laughter she had heard in the halls of the hotel.

"This is Pam Jones," Uncle Joe said again. "But she's better known as Rutherford Thackeray. That's the name she uses for the Gwen Gilderstar books."

Laura stared at the woman in disbelief. "You're Rutherford Thackeray?" she exclaimed. "You're engaged to Uncle Joe? You're my favorite writer!"

Pam Jones smiled, and for the first time Laura saw that she wasn't strange or ghostly at all. "Thank you," said Pam. "Your uncle told me that you read my books."

"Read them? She sleeps with them," added Bill.

Uncle Joe heaved a big sigh. "It sure was hard not to tell you about Pam," he said. "It was especially hard not to tell you, Laura! Every time I saw you with one of Pam's books, I wanted to tell you I knew her.

"Why didn't you?" asked Laura.

Pam's dark eyes looked kindly into Laura's eyes. "I'm afraid it's my fault," she confessed. "I didn't want anyone to know about the wedding. I want to get married quietly. If the press finds out about Joe and me, they'll ruin our plans. Can you imagine getting married with reporters snooping for details?"

"But why couldn't you tell us?" she asked.

"I'm sorry," said Pam. "I just didn't want anyone to know until right before the wedding. It's the only way to keep a secret."

"Is that why you sent Aunt Gigi away?" Bill asked.

Uncle Joe nodded. "She was starting to suspect something," he said. "And you know how Gigi can't keep a secret."

Pretending to be serious, Laura asked, "Should we call you Aunt Pam, Aunt Princess, or Aunt Rutherford Thackeray?"

Pam laughed, and this time her laughter had a merry ring to it. Touching Laura lightly on the cheek, she spoke softly. "Why don't you and Bill call me Aunt Pam?" Then she looked happily at Uncle Joe, who was stroking his mustache thoughtfully.

"There are just a couple of things I can't figure out," said Bill. "Where did the organ music come from?"

"The music is from my cassette player," Pam explained. "I'd bring it with me when I was here making wedding plans. It's the music we'll play at the wedding. But for the wedding there will be a big organ brought in, and it'll sound much better."

"And why did the painting fall off the wall?" asked Laura.

Pam thought for a moment. "Oh," she said, remembering. "I was in the next room where our reception will be. I was hanging a flower basket on the wall to get a better idea of how the room would look with some fixing up. The hammering caused the picture to fall."

Laura pointed to the bouquet of red roses in Pam's hand. "We found a rose by the princess' picture. It was really creepy. Did you leave it there?" she asked.

"Yes," Pam nodded. "I dropped it. I picked it up later. I'll be decorating The Princess Room with red roses for the wedding. I wanted to get a feel for how things would look. I guess I was being overly romantic."

"Gee," said Laura. "We all must have been here at the same time."

Pam smiled. "I thought I heard someone," she confessed. "I admit I was a little afraid when I heard noises in this big old place."

Bill chuckled. "You were afraid?" he hooted. "We were terrified!"

"Was it you who made the security alarm go off?" asked Laura.

Pam nodded again. She looked apologetically at Uncle Joe. "I just wanted to see what the hotel looked like at night because we'll be having an evening candlelight ceremony. I never thought about the alarm."

"Were those your footsteps in the snow upstairs?" asked Bill.

Pam thought for a minute. "They must've

been," she said, looking a little puzzled.

"You see," explained Uncle Joe. "Snow gets into the rooms even with the windows shut because the hotel is so poorly insulated. That's why it's closed in the winter. It's just too darned cold."

"But what about all the stories we heard?" asked Laura. "Everyone around here has seen the princess or has heard about her."

Pam nodded. "There really was a princess at one time," she explained. "Legends and stories about her pop up all the time. I'm not sure how they got started. In fact, that's how Uncle Joe and I met one another. I live close to here, so I came into Brinkley to investigate the stories. I thought I might be able to use them in a mystery novel."

Pam smiled at Laura and then continued. "Your Uncle Joe agreed to take me on a tour of the hotel. I took notes for my story, and we had such a good time! We've been seeing each other secretly for almost three months."

Pam glanced at Uncle Joe. Laura couldn't

be sure, but it looked like her uncle was blushing. It was strange to see a grown man acting so mushy.

"What are you going to tell Aunt Gigi?" asked Laura. "She's coming home today, isn't she?"

Uncle Joe looked worried. "I'll just tell her the truth," he said. "And hopefully she'll keep our secret."

Ten

L ATER that afternoon, everyone gathered around Uncle Joe's fireplace to hear Aunt Gigi's stories. Laura still couldn't believe that the writer of the Gwen Gilderstar books was going to be a part of her family!

Aunt Gigi pulled her chair closer to the hearth. "It's good to be home," she said. Her red hair glowed in the firelight. Gazing fondly at everyone, she said, "Well, at least we get to spend one evening together."

Uncle Joe looked guiltily at his sister as he sat quietly holding Pam's hand. "I'm sorry," he apologized. "It seemed like the only way to keep our wedding plans quiet."

"Wild horses couldn't drag your secret out of me!" Aunt Gigi said sternly.

Laura could barely stifle a giggle at that. "And believe me, I know some people who would just die if they knew about you and Pam. Mable Orkins is one of them," Aunt Gigi said.

Aunt Gigi caught her breath. "But don't worry," she added hastily, darting a look at Uncle Joe and Pam. "Your secret's safe with me."

Aunt Gigi leaned back in her chair, staring happily at the ceiling. "I'll bet that this is the biggest news to hit Brinkley in years!" she said. "Your wedding will make this sleepy old town sit up and take notice. I can't wait!"

Uncle Joe smiled at Aunt Gigi. He squeezed Pam's hand and glanced lovingly at her. Then, looking back at Aunt Gigi, he grinned and said, "Well, you'll have to keep our secret until spring. We're planning an April wedding."

"I hope that all of you can come back to Brinkley for the big event," Pam said.

Laura's heart leapt with excitement. "Can we, Mom?" she asked eagerly.

Mrs. Bingman smiled and nodded her head.

"Of course, we can. We wouldn't miss the wedding for the world," she said.

Bill stabbed at a log in the fireplace with a poker. "Remember all the ghost stories you told us around this fireplace, Uncle Joe?" he asked "You practically scared Laura out of her shoes!"

"What?" Laura shot her brother a frown. "I wasn't the one who was afraid," she said. "You're the one who didn't want to go into the hotel in the first place. You were chicken!"

"Ha!" hooted Bill. "You were the one who wanted to run away when we first saw the elevator moving. And you're the one who practically fainted when we saw the picture of the princess in the tower."

Laura pointed an accusing finger. "You're the one who saw Pam in the elevator and said she was the princess. You even said that she was holding an ax!"

Pam looked at Bill and said, "I was carrying a hammer to check some of the decorations for the reception. You must have seen the reflection off the top of the hammer and thought it was an ax."

Bill looked embarrassed. He ran his fingers through his hair. "Next time you're trying to solve a mystery, count me out," he grumbled. "I don't want to have anything to do with your mysteries."

Mr. Bingman's voice was serious. "You kids are lucky you didn't get hurt," he said. "You know you shouldn't have been wandering all over that hotel alone."

Uncle Joe patted his brother-in-law on the back. "It's okay now," he said. "I've made sure everything is locked up tight. And all the windows are locked, too," he said, grinning at Laura and Bill. "It's so secure that a shadow couldn't slip into that place!"

Laura's eyes cast a questioning look at Uncle Joe and Pam. "What about all of those stories about the princess?" she asked. "Do you think Mrs. Natch's husband really saw her ghost?"

Pam looked thoughtful. "No one knows,"

she said. "There are so many tales and legends that it certainly makes you wonder. Besides the princess, there's supposed to be another ghost roaming the hotel. This ghost wears a coonskin cap." She smiled at Uncle Joe, who shook his head.

Pam continued. "People around here talk about an explorer and trapper named Cal Killoway who helped to settle this area back in the mid-1700s.

Laura listened intently. She saw Bill was scooting in closer to hear.

"They say Cal Killoway died up in the mountains when he was looking for gold," Pam continued. "Legend has it that his ghost went mad and began hunting people instead of animals."

Laura shivered.

Pam's voice grew soft. "People at the hotel claim to see Cal Killoway from time to time," she continued. "A few years ago, a guest screamed in the middle of the night. Security guards rushed to her room. She said that a man in a coonskin cap and buckskins had come into her room. Then he vanished through a wall."

"Hey, maybe the weird guy that Bill and I saw in the steam room was Cal Killoway!" Laura said.

Uncle Joe looked at Laura and said, "Maybe it was. You never know around here."

"Don't get Laura started," Bill warned. "First thing you know she'll be getting an army of ghost busters together. And I know she'll try to drag me into it!"

Laura sighed. "We're leaving tomorrow morning, anyway," she reminded her brother. "I don't have time to solve another mystery."

When morning arrived, Laura heard the hustle and bustle in the house around her. Sounds of her parents packing the car drifted up the stairway. She quickly dressed and went downstairs for breakfast. From across the table, Laura watched her uncle. It seemed funny to have suspected he was being haunted by a ghost. I guess being in love is kind of like being haunted, Laura reasoned.

When everyone had finished eating, the Bingmans piled into their car. Laura gave Aunt Gigi and Uncle Joe one last hug and climbed into the backseat beside Bill.

"Move over," growled Bill. "And try to keep on your side of the seat."

"Some things never change," Laura mumbled under her breath.

Laura waved good-bye to Uncle Joe and Aunt Gigi as the Bingmans' car pulled from the driveway into the street. She looked out the side window and saw the Royal Windmont Hotel. The hotel definitely was as elegant, huge, and mysterious as ever.

As Laura peered at the tower, she saw a figure moving. Then she saw someone—or something—wave. Startled, she turned toward her brother. "Look, Bill!" she exclaimed. "There's someone in the tower!"

"Oh, no," Bill moaned. "Not this again."

Laura continued to stare at the tower window until her dad slowly steered the car

around the next bend.

"I saw somebody waving!" Laura insisted, turning to face Bill. "I swear I did."

"It was probably Pam," Bill said. "You know how she's always around the hotel planning the wedding. That's the only person it could be. Remember Uncle Joe said the hotel is locked up tight?"

Laura nodded and leaned back in her seat. *Here I go again*, she reminded herself. *I just can't help it when there might be a mystery.*

Laura decided to ignore Bill as her dad drove through the town of Brinkley. She looked at the shops that lined both sides of the street. Suddenly, Mr. Bingman honked the car's horn and waved. Laura turned quickly to see Pam climbing into her car. She held a big package under one arm. She waved back with the other hand.

Before Laura had a chance to respond, the town was behind them, and their drive back to Indiana had begun. Laura's mind was spinning. *It couldn't have been Pam waving from the hotel tower. So, who was it?*

A little shiver ran through Laura, and the hair on the back of her neck prickled with excitement. She couldn't be sure, but the person in the tower seemed to have something on its head. *Could it have been a coonskin cap?*

She tried to settle into her seat. Her mind whirled with all the possibilities. She couldn't wait to come back in April. Perhaps there was a mystery in Brinkley, after all.

About the Author

"I remember what it was like to be a kid," says JANET ADELE BLOSS. "I understand how kids feel things."

Anyone who reads Janet's books will agree that she has a keen insight into the emotional lives of children. The characters in her books live in a kids' world of pesty sisters, creepy brothers, runaway pets, school bullies, and good friends.

Janet showed signs of becoming an author as early as third grade when she wrote a story entitled *Monkeys on the Moon.* She also wanted to become a flamenco dancer, a spy, a skater for roller derby, and a beach bum in California. But fortunately for her readers it was the dream of becoming an author that came true.

Although Janet's first love is writing ,her other interests include dancing, music, camping, swimming, ice-skating, and cats.